The Prison Planet

The Prison Planet

Luis Chester

Book Two - Hidden in the Lapses of Time

There is a hidden truth about life on Earth.

The apparent path everyone follows is, in reality, a carefully implanted illusion—one designed to make you believe this is how life is supposed to be.

From a young age, I observed the people around me, even my own parents.

Their lives seemed per-programmed: Go to school to learn things you already intuitively know.

Get a job working for a corporation.

Find your "other half" and get married.

Have children.

Take on a mortgage for a dream house—or one that isn't quite a dream.

Buy a car.

Reach retirement age.

Die alone in a care home where your children have placed you.

What's wrong with this picture?

This thought haunted me.

I couldn't shake it.

This book is another work of fiction—yet within it lies a deeper truth.

Our character is about to uncover the reality behind this rationalized way of living.

It is a sequel to my first book, The Timeless Soulmates – Ode to Eternal Love.

Are you ready for that truth to be revealed?

If you too feel like something doesn't make sense... Keep reading.

You may just wake up to the reality of this so-called planet Earth.

Look out.

You are being observed.

—The author

Back to the Original Plan

Fer found himself with a half-broken heart.

The last call from Eve had taken him by surprise.

"I like you as a friend, but I don't see you as the man I want to live with."

Suddenly, his world shattered.

Nothing mattered more to him than her.

Sitting in his car, still reeling from the news, he started to drive.

No destination in mind—just forward motion.

With cruise control engaged, Fer was only physically present to avoid crashing into others.

His mind was lost in that phone call.

Time passed.

Eventually, he realized he was crossing the Channel Tunnel. France was just a few miles away.

His thoughts drifted to the original plan—one he had conceived long before meeting Eve.

When the gas tank emptied, he pulled off the road, leaving behind everything, even the car keys.

And just like that, he started walking.

Not long after, he found himself booking a seat on the legendary Orient Express.

Destination: Japan.

Then, the Tibetan Plateau.

Run for Your Life

A new day arrived.

Fer stood at the window of the small inn, gazing out at the city.

In the distance, the Ivory Tower pierced the skyline—a silent sentinel watching over all.

On the old wooden dresser lay his passport, visas, and a scatter of currencies from different lands, ready for the road ahead.

Sadness crept over his face as a final thought of Eve slipped through.

"The end of my last days is waiting."

"Let's go back home."

Seated in his cabin aboard the historic train, Fer felt his life unfold before him like a silent film.

A whistle cut through the morning air.

The journey had begun, rumbling through borders and landscapes on its way east toward Asia.

As the outskirts of Paris faded behind him, Fer knew: there was no turning back.

"Goodbye, my love. See you in the next life."

With that, he erased every lingering memory of his present life.

Now, his focus was fixed on one destination—the vast Tibetan Plateau, where the Yellow River had flowed for thousands of years.

Nightfall crept in, and the horizon burned with the fire-colored glow of a descending sun.

Suddenly, the door to Fer's cabin opened and slammed shut again in an instant.

A man had entered—his presence fast, silent, and cloaked in shadow.
A chill ran through Fer.
That energy.
That darkness. "
They're coming for me. Again."

The Past Persuasion

Once again, Fer found himself hiding from the echoes of his past lives.

In one of them, he was Liu Shong, a warrior from ancient Japan.

But something had gone wrong.

Instead of moving toward the light after death, Liu had drifted the other way—pulled back into Earth by a powerful tether.

He was reborn into a baby boy... but retained the memories of his former life.

He remembered Aki.

His beloved.

Liu's early childhood with Aki was filled with joy.

As he grew, he followed a traditional path—trained in the art of the samurai, like his father before him.

His education was passed down with discipline and honor.

But it didn't take long for his father to see that Liu was different.

At a sacred ceremony under the full moon, Liu was raised to the heavens—the family's declaration that the Chosen One had arrived.

And slowly, it became clear.

He knew things no child should know.

Skills no training had yet taught him.

The knowledge of past lives already lived within him.

Honor. Respect. Integrity.

These were the core virtues of a samurai.

Swordsmanship was merely the surface.

But Liu surpassed them all.

Then, he started to notice it: a presence in the shadows.

A movement too fast for the eye.

A feeling too dark to ignore.

Something—or someone—was watching.

Why?

Because Liu had escaped the reincarnation system.

In the ordinary cycle, the body dies, and your soul is beamed upward to a station of implants.

There, a new lifetime is assigned, and you're sent back to Earth—reborn, mind wiped, ready to try again.

But what if you break that loop?

What if, like Liu, you slip through the cracks?

You remain... you remember.

And though it's disorienting at first, the results are remarkable. Fer—now in the 21st century—carries the brilliance and abilities of 33 past lives.

A level of awareness that exceeds all but a fraction of the greatest minds alive.

But now, as the train races forward, he feels their presence again—those prison guardians.

They can't touch him while he's embodied.

But they've found ways before... manipulation, accidents, even staged deaths to force his exit—and beam him up.

This time, it's life or death. Again.

And Fer knows he might not win. If he loses, all his lifetimes—all 33—will be wiped clean.

Erased forever.

And what else?

Only God knows.

He reaches for an old suitcase—recovered from a hidden safe house, preserved through lifetimes.

Inside: photographs, artifacts, documents… even fragments of furniture.

Among them, the samurai vest of his father, resting on a wooden stand.

And the weapon.

A portable laser sword—crafted using the knowledge of a distant star-faring civilization.

"Ready for it."

"Game on."

Life or Death

The Orient Express had long since left France behind.

Fer now moved shadow to shadow, teleportation through the folds of space and time—his speed imperceptible to the human eye.

It was an ancient technique, inherited from the Japanese ninjas—one that allowed him to slip through temporal lapses without being detected.

Time was critical.

He had no intention of leaving the train—that would have been the easier escape, but also a retreat.

He intended to reach the Tibetan Plateau.

And he would do it aboard this train.

During one of these temporal jumps, he sensed it.

Another presence—trying to occupy the same pocket of space.

It was time. In a flash, he activated his combat device.

A beam of laser light struck the being behind him.

A burst of energy flared and extinguished in the same instant.

"One less," Fer thought coldly.

Later that night, the portly conductor shuffled through first class.

He paused, confused, spotting a tiny pile of fine ash in the aisle.

"Huh. That wasn't here before…"

One Lifetime Before

Finally, Fer allowed himself to close his eyes.

The train pressed forward, slicing through the icy winter air as it rolled across foreign landscapes.

His thoughts turned inward—to the most pivotal lifetime before this one.

The memories were as vivid as the present.

Location: Wales, near the northern border with England.

"From a very early age, I dreamed of becoming an elite pilot in the Macab Galactic Confederation."

But in that society, he had been born into one of the lowest castes. And in such a system, ascension was forbidden.

Let alone admission into the elite ranks of the galaxy.

"But I knew who I was. I am a powerful being.

And I was going to overcome that wall."

He became the best—top of his class, earning rare commendations, outshining every peer.

When the day finally came, he submitted his application. RE-FUSED—printed in bold.

In the midst of that devastation, he saw her.

The Captain's daughter. Golden hair, sculpted figure, wrapped in perfectly tailored silk.

Laughing, carefree.

He put on his finest smile and adopted the poise of the elite.

He approached her with confidence.

Months later, they were married.

There was no love—not really. But love wasn't his goal.

Access was.

And with that marriage came admission into the elite pilot program.

That strategy worked... for a while.

In that lifetime, named Fer once again, ambition eclipsed everything.

He climbed higher.

I want more.

Another woman.

Another status.

Another marriage.

Another victory.

But inside... It felt heavy.

His betrayal of a good woman—the second one—haunted him.

He had traded truth for status.

Love for ambition.

He lost his self-determination. T

hen, during one argument—nothing more than a few harsh words—he snapped.

climbed into his red sports car and sped furiously through Wales' narrow, twisting roads.

The roar of the engine echoed his fury.

When he saw the ancient tree just off the bend... he didn't swerve.

The crash was cataclysmic.

Thrown from the wreck, his body was broken.

An English hospital became his tomb of recovery.

He awoke days later—wrapped in casts, bandaged and still.

A young nurse greeted him with soft eyes. "Hi... do you know where you are?"

He gently shook his head.

No idea.

No name.

No past.

And—no control of his legs.

With no identification, no license plate, no history to trace, the staff gave him a name: John Smith.

The most generic name they could find.

Days bled into weeks—until, one day, a man entered the ward.

Tall, kindly, with a stethoscope in hand and a quiet strength in his eyes.

"I'm looking for patients to test a new approach in mental recovery," he said.

"Would you be willing to work with me?"

Fer remembered the name: Dr. Lafayette.

Within months, he was walking again.

His memories returned.

And he achieved what the doctor called a new level of awareness.

Fer never returned to his former life.

He stayed with the man who had saved him—and learned to help others as he had been helped.

Tears ran down his face as the train rumbled on.

"Farewell, my friend," he whispered softly.

"I hope to see you again—on another planet, in another life, in another civilization."

Asia on the Horizon

This was Fer's last stop.

The final station before reaching the threshold of Tibet.

Winter had begun to settle in, and he knew the road ahead would be long and unforgiving.

He gathered the minimal gear he'd need—clothing and tools to brave the colossal obstacles ahead.

No map.

No electronic devices.

Only his memory, sharpened across centuries, would guide him.

Landmarks remained—etched into Earth's bones.

Even though the landscape had changed, some features were eternal.

Wrapped in an old piece of woven cloth, his samurai sword rested against his back—his quiet companion.

Dressed in dark, practical clothing and unusual footwear for the cold, he stepped into the wild, leaving behind the last shadows of civilization.

Two months passed.

He traveled through breathtaking landscapes, avoiding main roads and border patrols.

His path was solitary, but not lonely.

Each step brought him closer.

At last, he looked up—toward the massive mountain before him.

Below it, the Yellow River surged, roaring through ancient rock like a cry that had never stopped.

Fer began to see it... the plateau.
His old home.
The field.
The place where, 33 lifetimes ago, he had lived with Aki.
He touched the grass—soft and thawing under the sun's warmth.
A small flower bloomed, defiant in the lingering snow.
He closed his eyes, and for a moment, it was all there again: Aki.
Crossing the field.
Carrying vegetables in her shawl.
Smiling toward him.
His heart swelled.
Time folded.
"I'm here again, my eternal love."

Life Changes Forever

The man known as Fer... no longer existed.

He sat once more on the Tibetan Plateau, alone but whole—surrounded by silence, warmed by the sun, at peace.

In England, Eve clutched the memory book he had left behind.

She read it again.

And again.

And again.

Each page woke something in her.

And with it, came her own buried memories—rising like mist.

Fer, gazing across his old fields at the start of a new day, noticed something.

A figure.

He stood.

Someone had entered his sacred space.

He narrowed his eyes.

A woman.

Bending to pick vegetables, just as Aki once had.

It couldn't be.

Could it?

He ran—faster than time.

Stopping several paces away, breath caught.

"Eve?"

She lifted her gaze.

Beautiful.

Familiar.

"Fer?"

"I missed seeing you. I missed hugging you." They fell into each other's arms like two pieces of the same soul—trying to become one.

"I'm back too," she whispered.

"My soulmate."

Time passed.

A new home rose—built where the old one had stood.

The land gave generously, as if it had been waiting for them.

They needed nothing more.

Inside, they sat facing each other on the floor.

Fingers intertwined.

Touching, loving—physically, spiritually.

They laughed, they cried.

They rediscovered each other like explorers returning home.

And in their love, the physical universe began to surrender.

It couldn't contain what they had become.

They were too strong.

Because love—love is the key.

Book Three – The Ultimate
Sacrifice

"The future is dreamed by artists."
This is the third volume in a sequence of ten.
Don't miss the next chapter in the extraordinary lives of Eve and Fer.
Something dramatic is about to unfold.
Are they prepared for the unimaginable sacrifice?
Turn the page and find out...
—The Author

The Thread

Life continued peacefully on the Tibetan Plateau as winter settled in once again.

Fer and Eve lived in harmony, their love deepening with each passing day.

Their bond transcended words, yet they never missed a chance to say it: "I LOVE YOU!!!"

Each day.

Every night.

Like a ritual.

One night, as they lay wrapped in each other's arms, the sky above was breathtaking—clear and endless.

The Star of Macab shimmered overhead.

Mars and Venus stood proudly beside it, like silent witnesses.

Then, a sound.

Low, distant at first.

A rumble echoing from the nearby mountains.

Fer opened his eyes.

He reached for Eve. "Something's not right," he whispered.

The noise grew louder, thunderous.

Fer grabbed Eve's hand and pulled her beneath the doorway's timber frame—the strongest point of their small cabin.

Seconds later, a massive wave of snow slammed into the structure, shaking the walls and swallowing the room in ice and silence.

Stillness returned.

But it was unnatural.

Fer stirred.

He reached beside him—no hand.

No Eve. Panic struck.

He began to dig, clawing at the packed snow, his breath shallow, heart hammering.

Breaking through to the surface, he gasped for air, snow clinging to his skin.

There was only one thought.

Find her.

He turned, digging frantically, when something shifted behind him.

A presence.

Dark.

Human in shape.

And in its hand, a weapon—one Fer recognized.

A soul-capturing device from another world.

His senses sharpened.

And then he saw it. Eve—her soul—being lifted.

Beamed upward, caught inside a trap he had once escaped.

"NOoooo!" He lunged.

The being vanished like smoke.

Fer collapsed into the snow, hands gripping his skull, heart broken open to the void.

"Why, Eve?

Take me, you bastard!" he sobbed.

Above, the stars still shimmered.

But for Fer, the night had never been darker.

The Trap

The first light of day crept across the horizon.

Fer hadn't moved.

Then, like a bolt of lightning, realization struck.

"I know how to deceive these creatures," he thought.

Reversing course, he pulled himself back down into the snow-filled hole he had dug the night before, submerging himself deeper—swimming downward through the frozen layers.

It didn't take long before his body began to shut down.

The brutal cold numbed him quickly.

Somewhere far from Earth, deep within a distant planetary station, a sudden alert broke routine.

On a control screen above the Tibetan Plateau, a soul signature flickered into view.

Fer's soul hovered above the snow-covered cabin.

The trap activated.

In a beam of brilliant light, he was pulled into the sterile interior of an electronic capture chamber.

Fer—let's keep calling him that—played his part, feigning disorientation.

"I must wait. The right moment will come."

On the other side of the vast Martian complex, the Big Hunter team—the same group that had chased him through lifetimes—received the alert.

"Don't put him in front of the screen!" one shouted.

But it was too late.

By the time they arrived, the rookie implanter had already completed Fer's new life assignment and forced him to look at it.

Fer turned.

He saw them standing at the door.

He smiled.

"Perfect timing."

With centuries of knowledge behind him, Fer triggered the mental escape routine.

He broke the imprinting pattern and slipped out of the trap.

"Time to find Eve," he whispered.

Finding Eve

Alarms blared across the Martian base.

The Big Hunter team rushed to the armory, grabbing portable tracking and capture devices.

Each member shot off in a different direction, warping through the rifts of time.

Fer, meanwhile, moved through space undetected—hiding between dimensional folds, avoiding pursuit while desperately seeking Eve.

But her presence wasn't there.

"Where have they taken her?" he asked aloud.

"Is there another system I've never known?"

Then, a whisper of recognition brushed his senses.

Risking exposure, Fer traveled to the outer magnetic boundary of Mars.

And there he saw it—her. Eve's soul, bound inside an electronic containment box.

"He took the bait!" a Hunter barked.

"Now we've got him."

A new trap had been laid.

And Fer walked straight into it.

He was seized and confined—locked inside another soul box, then hurled down into the planetary gravity well.

A precision trap, designed around his only weakness: Love.

Time passed.

Though time itself had no meaning anymore. T

he Hunters thought he was broken.

That he'd submit.

They were wrong.

Fer focused inward.

He began analyzing the trap's nature, applying the fundamental principles of this sector of the universe—axioms he'd once studied.

"Why didn't I think of this earlier?"

"This universe operates on terminals—polarities.

If I can create a second terminal, a mirrored construct, I'll break the containment."

He looked at the blank whiteness of the trap.

In his mind, he built a twin—black, identical, and opposite.

Suddenly—he was free.

He sent the concept through the ether, and Eve followed his mental design.

Moments later, her soul burst from the trap as well.

They reunited above the red planet.

There was no time to celebrate.

The Hunters would be back.

They had to leave—now.

The Declared War in the Stars

Not far from Earth, in the direction of the star known as the Sun, a massive space complex orbited in secrecy.

Inside, newly formed beings—still inactive—waited.

Their singular purpose: to gather knowledge from all beings living within the Macab Galactic Confederation and use that data to build a civilization of perfect order.

Earth, with its diversity and deep spiritual roots, had long been under observation.

One of these collectors had lived among humans for millennia—returning life after life in new forms.

Small in stature to blend in, this being made contact with the planet's earliest spiritual masters.

It began with the Vedas.

Continued through the life of Siddhartha Gautama.

Each time, new wisdom was delivered back to the civilization's main archive—hidden beneath the radiant clouds of Venus.

Now, Fer and Eve arrived at that Venusian complex.

"This place..." Eve whispered, gazing at her surroundings.

"The bodies here aren't made of flesh," Fer explained.

"They're mechanical.

Durable.

Eternal.

No need for sustenance or sleep."

Together, they selected new forms.

"Come with me," Fer said.

"I'll show you around."

They entered a vast chamber where Venus's wisest minds telepathically exchanged knowledge.

The space buzzed with silent brilliance.

Eve stared, astonished, at how naturally Fer moved among them.

He shared everything—his capture on Mars, the traps, the soul box, the stolen memories.

The manipulation continued.

Earth's population was still imprisoned.

One of the elders responded. "Something similar happened before." A halo-recording played: a facility like the one on Mars, disintegrated by a Venusian fleet long ago.

"So... they rebuilt it," Fer said grimly.

"And they're still enslaving that population."

Venus received and recorded the data.

Rotations of the Sun passed.

The decision was unanimous.

War was declared on the deceivers—those vicious manipulators known as the Psycho.

The war in the stars had begun.

The Way Out of the Earth Prison

Tibet – circa 1043 BC

A small collector from Venus made its way along a narrow mountain path toward a monastery.

It was morning.

Cold, but golden with sunlight.

Suddenly, silence shattered—an avalanche crashed down the slope.

The being's mechanical body was crushed beneath stone.

Hovering above the wreckage, its soul detached.

Then—a pull.

Beamed away, it found itself trapped in the infamous Mars complex.

An implant procedure had begun.

A glowing round screen tried to force data into its consciousness.

But it didn't work.

This being was different.

The Big Psycho was called in.

He studied the data.

The subject was... not from the enslaved race.

In a panic, the Psycho sealed the soul inside an electronic soul box and cast it into Mars's magnetic field—eternal containment.

But even that wasn't enough.

The Venusian broke free.

Using fundamental axioms of the universe, like Fer later would, it escaped and returned home with crucial intel.

Venus acted swiftly. A

fleet was dispatched through a wormhole.

They reached Mars.

Laser beams cut through the surface.

The complex was erased.

Back on Venus, the being was summoned before the highest council.

"These beings deserve freedom," he said.

"They are not criminals—they are rebels.

Architects. Dreamers. Artists. Like us."

"But you'll be alone if you return," one warned.

"If the Confederation learns of this—"

"Then so be it," he said.

They gave him their blessing.

He went back—to Earth.

And life after life, he gathered knowledge.

Studied the body.

Studied the traps.

Studied the lies.

Then, a breakthrough.

Using universal axioms, he uncovered the root implant—the great lie that initiated planetary amnesia.

He built a path.

A protocol.

A system of liberation.

The Path.

He discovered even more—about himself, about the universe, about all souls... even his Venusian kin.

He found the way back to Be

Back to the Planet

With the full knowledge of his past lives now restored, Fer was ready.

He and Eve returned to Earth—no longer as fugitives, but as leaders among the growing resistance.

All around the planet, souls were waking up.

The war in the stars had shattered the veil.

Nothing was hidden anymore.

Spaceships appeared openly in the skies.

The lies had crumbled.

The traps exposed.

"We are here to reclaim the abilities we once held," Fer declared.

"When the wise samurai raised me—Liun, Fer, it no longer matters—and proclaimed, 'The Expected One is born. Bow before him, moon,' I never imagined it would come to this."

Eve looked at him, eyes burning with purpose.

"The future is among the stars. We're waiting for you." Fer smiled gently.

"Will you come to join us?"

Book Four – Futures Past's Impingement

Our past influences us—right here, right now.

Do you agree?

If past lives are real...

Can they reach forward and steer our current decisions?

Join Fer and Eve as they confront not just alien forces and spiritual truths, but echoes of their own unfinished choices—bleeding through time to affect the present.

The question isn't only who we are... but who we once were.

Are your actions today your own?

Or are they the ripple of something long ago decided?

Ready?

Let's go.

—The Author

In a Far, Far Future Time

Fer is surrounded by young cadets preparing to become planetary leaders.

Earth has changed drastically.

Once known as the Prison Planet, it's now the base of a newly established order responsible for cleansing the other 75 habitable planets in this sector of the galaxy from vicious creatures.

Most of us migrated to other planets—ironically, the same ones we were once exiled from.

The War in the Stars has reached its climax.

Fer and Eve are legends here.

Even in their new bodies, they chose to keep their previous names.

Though they've cycled through infancy, adolescence, and adulthood again, their memories remain untouched.

Whenever Fer walks past the academy, young cadets swarm him.

They know who he is.

They beg to hear his stories.

Today is no exception.

"Would you like to know how a decision I made over a million years ago changed my life forever?"

A unanimous "YES" erupts.

Fer sits, and the group gathers around him on the floor.

"At that time, a new order had just formed in this sector of the galaxy.

Advanced technology allowed us to build immense cities on the planet Macab.

The discovery of clean propulsion revolutionized space travel, sparking agreements between the various species living here.

Then, a recently arrived species began to infiltrate the upper echelons of the Macab Confederation government—subtly, serpent-like.

Their first success in the High Congress was the creation of a caste system.

'Not everyone is born equal.'

It was a poisonous idea, slowly planted in the minds of the population.

When I was born," Fer continued, "my parents were classified as part of an inferior caste—restricted to menial labor.

We lived underground. 'You are not entitled to see the daylight,' they told us.

But I was different.

I rejected this imposed reality.

Something didn't make sense.

The societal implant that bound everyone had no effect on me.

Do you know why?"

"Yes," one cadet responded.

"You're part of a newer species in this sector—the old implant didn't influence you."

"Exactly. I could see how hypnotized they all were.

Even my parents.

They obeyed orders without question.

As a child, I became the 'slave' of a boy from a superior caste.

On the surface, we grew close—he was around my age.

He allowed me to study beside him: law, physics, and the most fascinating subject of all—spaceship piloting. It became clear that I needed to escape that planet and its cruel society.

I knew I'd been born in the wrong place at the wrong time.

My species was out there.

Somewhere.

And I was right.

Whether through luck or sheer will, I was eventually permitted to attend advanced classes.

Every day, I completed all my tasks—waking early, preparing for the teacher's arrival.

The old man was calm, and maybe a rebel himself in his youth.

He took notice of me. I learned fast.

One morning, before class began, I drew the schematic of the newest propulsion system on the magnetic board—formulas and all.

I even proposed an upgrade: using lapses in time to make spatial 'jumps'.

The teacher was amazed.

He looked at me and said, 'You're one of the cleverest students I've ever taught.'

Somehow—I'm still not sure how—I was invited to compete in contests against students from other planets.

I consistently earned top honors.

After one award ceremony, a Master granted me the chance to speak to the assembly.

He asked, 'What would you like to be in the future?'

I answered instantly: 'I want to be an Elite Pilot of the Confederation.'

The audience burst out laughing—mockingly.

'The inferior one wants to ascend to the superior caste.'

I ran.

Dark thoughts began to fester inside me.

The confusion ignited something.

From then on, I had one goal: I would become an Elite Pilot of the Confederation.

No matter what it took.

That moment marked my descent into the realm of shadows.

A voice in my mind began to guide me.

But for now—back to our lessons.

I promise to continue next time."

All the kids—including Fer's daughter—wore the same expression.
"Why..."

The Consequent Decision

Some time had passed.

Fer was dispatched on a mission to one of the most distant planets—something wasn't right.

He arrived in his personal spacecraft, dressed in a pristine uniform complete with a white hat, strikingly similar to the 21st-century US Navy.

It was time to rejoin his pupils and resume advanced training.

As Fer approached the class space, the children spotted him and ran toward him.

"You promised to continue the story," one of them cried.

"Will you tell me today?" asked Fer's daughter.

She had grown up hearing the tales of her proud father, but Fer's retelling always came with fresh emotion and vivid intensity.

"Everyone take your seats," Fer said.

"Today's story will be part of our studies.

It will help you understand what we're still dealing with on other planets—like the one I've just returned from."

"Yes! It can be part of our exam," said another cadet eagerly.

"Alright then," Fer agreed.

"Now—where did I leave off?"

"You ran away from the graduation stage," his daughter replied instantly.

"Very good.

That moment became an obsession for me.

I started neglecting my duties.

I became cruel to those around me.

Secretly, I did bad things. I was spiraling toward disaster.

Years had passed since I scrubbed the booths for Sam—the 'rich' kid. It was supper time.

Captain Number One of the Elite Force had been invited to dinner at Sam's family estate, along with his wife and daughter.

I noticed the blonde girl watching me closely.

I continued my tasks.

After dinner, most guests lingered indoors, chatting.

She stepped outside—looking for something, or someone.

I nearly collided with her.

Her name was Sonya.

'A thousand apologies, my lady,' I stammered, hoping to avoid punishment.

She looked directly at me.

'Aren't you the boy who received that big commendation on stage?'

I hesitated, unsure whether I was allowed to look up.

But she softened.

'It's alright. You are, aren't you?'

I nodded quietly.

She took my hand—and we ran outside.

It felt magical.

I sensed that she liked me.

In fact, Sonya was in love with me.

We began to meet in quiet corners of the house.

She grew closer to Sam just to be near me.

But my motives turned darker.

For her, it was a simple crush—a playful game of seduction.

For me, it was an opportunity.

I played the game masterfully.

Eventually, she fell under my spell. The lamb had been caught by the wolf.

I nudged her to speak to her father about my brilliance.

And soon enough, I stood before the Captain himself.

Using my skills, I presented him with a bold wartime tactic.

He was impressed.

We became close—he introduced me to others in the Force's inner circle.

One day, when we were alone, I looked him in the eye. 'I want to marry your daughter.'

He stared at me, then burst into laughter.

It felt like history was repeating itself.

I turned slowly toward the door, head bowed.

Then he said— 'I've been expecting this for a long time.'

'Of course you have my approval.'

16

Outside the Comfort Zone

Eve stood silently at the glass door.

Fer noticed her and motioned gently for her to come inside.

Leya, their daughter, lit up with joy at the sight of her mother.

The entire class buzzed with excitement—they knew Eve was Fer's soulmate, the woman who helped ignite the War in the Stars and unlock Earth's prison gates.

"Can we step outside?" Eve asked softly.

They slid through the door together.

"Tell me, my love," Fer said, gazing at her like an innocent boy in love.

She glanced around, then kissed him warmly when no one was watching.

"Wow," he whispered, caught off guard by her passion.

"What's going on?"

"Fer, I've been invited on a new mission to a primitive planet at the edge of the Confederation. It's important, and I want to go.

I'll be grateful to guide them—teach them the basics, the communication cycle, the triangle of understanding.

Will you be alright if I leave?"

Fer's eyes sparkled with pride.

"Of course. I know how deeply you believe in freeing civilizations. Go."

He kissed her again, without restraint.

She smiled—for the shared understanding that defined their life together.

As she walked away, Fer watched her fondly. "Keep that beautiful body in shape, alright?"

She turned and teased, "Don't look at me that way.

I know exactly what you're thinking."

Fer smirked. "I know. See you soon, my love."

Back in class, Fer noticed the cadets imitating his kiss.

"Very funny," he said, chuckling.

"Let's get back to it." The students settled in quietly, ready to listen.

"After Sonya's father approved our union, the process of caste ascension began.

Time passed—and the wedding day arrived.

Thought it was the best option to reach my goal,

I felt guilty.

I had no love for Sonya.

She was merely a tool.

But with that union, I entered the Confederation's Pilot Force.

I drilled constantly on the simulator.

That obsession never left me—I had to be exceptional to gain acceptance.

I ignored Sonya.

Never visited her.

Never took her calls.

But that wasn't the end.

I was a man—with desires. I noticed a beautiful pilot.

She was new.

She didn't know my past.

Again, I pushed myself to impress her.

Driven by the same obsession that led to my first mistake.

One day, she stepped off her ship parked beside mine.

I approached her from behind, spun her gently, and kissed her.

She resisted, but I had already woven my trap.

We entered a forbidden relationship—violating both pilot code and my vows.

That was the moment my integrity shattered.

From that point on, I was no longer free from the grip of desire.

And something else awakened inside me—regret, shame, and slow self-destruction."

The Decision's Entrapment

In 1716, our character Fer—known in that life as Francois—was born into a farmer's family in the countryside.

As a child, life was simple and happy.

He spent his days playing with his sister and helping his mother feed the chickens and rabbits.

School was not easily accessible at the time.

Only his father, with a little education, managed to carve out moments from his exhausting workday to teach Francois the basics—how to write his name.

An old book at home began to capture Francois's attention.

Though he couldn't read it fully, its illustrations fueled his imagination.

Dressed in a white shirt and shorts held up by suspenders, he imagined himself as the hero of that story.

With a wooden stick as his sword, he created imaginary opponents to fight for a beautiful young woman.

Play or no play, he always saw himself escaping that rural life to fight for love.

By the age of fifteen, Francois's life shifted dramatically when his father took him to a grand mansion.

"My son, I must leave you here. This will be your new home. Please... grow well." Francois was confused.

Why would his father want him to stay?

As the old open carriage drove away, Francois, tears glistening in his green eyes, tried to run after him.

"Father! Don't leave me alone!"

A servant held him back.

"It's all right.

You'll eat well here.

I'll teach you," the man reassured him.

Francois soon grew into his new role—caring for the mansion's horses.

One day, while tending the stables, he discovered an old sword.

After finishing his chores, he practiced with it daily, still clinging to his boyhood fantasy of fighting for a lover.

Years passed. Francois became a strong and striking young man—small in stature, but with a lean, muscular frame.

One afternoon, riding a black horse across an open field, he gave the animal a good run.

Out of nowhere, a girl on a brown horse appeared, galloping straight towards him.

Francois did everything he could to avoid a collision, but her horse reared, throwing her to the ground.

He leapt from his horse and rushed to her side as her body hit the earth with a soft thud.

She moaned in pain, her pink elaborate dress now stained with green grass.

Kneeling, Francois extended a hand.

"Let me help you."

The girl, a beauty with long blonde hair, glared at him.

"Stupid boy!

Don't touch me!" she snapped, struggling to stand and regain her ladylike composure.

"You came out of nowhere!" she accused.

"So did you," he countered.

Mounting her horse, Charlene rode away, leaving Francois watching her retreating figure.

From that day on, Francois found himself riding through the same field daily, hoping for another encounter.

Unbeknownst to him, Charlene did the same, always finding excuses to ride there.

On one overcast afternoon, fate intervened again.

Their horses nearly collided, and Charlene lost her balance.

Before she could hit the muddy ground, Francois jumped from his horse and caught her in his arms.

Time seemed to stop.

Holding her close, he felt her warmth, her rapid heartbeat.

She felt the same—safe in his strong arms and against his firm chest.

"Are you planning to set me down?" she asked finally, her voice softer this time.

"Yes."

Their green eyes met like mirrors.

The sky opened, releasing a heavy rain.

Francois took off his shirt and held it over her head to shield her.

"There's a small wooden cabin over there.

Come with me," he said.

Inside, away from prying eyes and societal rules, desire overwhelmed them.

They made love on the cabin floor, a passion that became their secret routine.

But as Francois lay on his simple bed in the stables, an old thought crept into his mind—malicious and ambitious.

The way out of this "servant" life is to marry a woman of status...

One night, he stole fine clothes from the mansion's drawers.

Dressed like a gentleman, he rode to Charlene's estate.

His charm and carefully crafted lies convinced the household staff to aid their secret meetings.

In the grand salon, standing beside Charlene as her parents watched, she hinted that a child was growing inside her.

"The father is Francois," she confessed.

His scheme had worked.

Once again, in a different lifetime, Fer had climbed the social ladder—using love as his ladder's rungs.

But the victory was hollow.

Guilt consumed him.

To amend his betrayal, Francois became a passive, miserable man, obeying Charlene's every demand.

Their marriage decayed to the point where they slept in separate rooms.

Worse still, Francois began an affair with Charlene's cousin, a newly-wed.

What started as kisses in hidden garden corners escalated to late-night trysts.

One night, the cousin's husband caught them mid-act.

He stared at them, his expression cold. "I expect you to be in the field at 8 am.

Bring your sword," he said flatly, then shut the door.

At dawn, Francois faced him.

His years of secret practice made him confident.

The duel went well—until Francois's conscience intervened.

Who is truly without honor here? he thought.

In a moment of clarity, he let his opponent's blade pierce his body.

Collapsing to the ground, blood gushed as life drained from him.

In the distance, he saw Charlene running toward him.

With his last strength, he raised a hand in a gesture of apology.

High above his lifeless body, his soul felt weightless—free once more.

Time to restart again... A new body.

Why not in England this time?

18

The Old Galactic Order

Eve landed in a remote part of the planet, accompanied by a few fellow college explorers.

Together, they began the long trek to the nearest habitable compound.

It took time to learn the language of the natives.

Before arrival, she had studied their traditions, caste systems, and clothing styles to blend in.

Now, living among them, she observed the rhythms of their simple farm life.

But beneath the surface, she noticed a disturbing influence.

The people were under the control of a so-called "witch doctor"—an alien entity whose vicious creatures worked to corrupt this pure, budding civilization.

They distributed chemical medications and subtle hypnotic practices, embedding control under the guise of healing.

To gain acceptance, Eve and her group introduced themselves as travelers from a distant clan, seeking fertile land for farming.

They kept learning about this Viking-like culture—its heraldry, its codes, and its legends.

It didn't take long for Eve to detect the patterns of manipulation. The doctor's treatments and hypnosis weren't healing; they were entrapment.

So she formed a plan.

In the mountains nearby, she and her companions gathered a group of curious youths.

There, they opened a school to teach the basics of communication, critical, and self-awareness.

Daily drills helped sharpen their minds and awaken their spirits.

Word spread quickly.

Parents began attending, eager to see the changes in their children.

Slowly, lives improved.

Communities grew stronger.

But the "good doctor" saw his control slipping.

In desperation, he launched a smear campaign.

He claimed one of his patients had died because they chose Eve's teachings over his medications.

The fearful and the weak-minded, swayed by the insinuations, joined the doctor's rebellion.

Soon, Eve and her group were ordered to leave the clan—they were no longer welcome.

Instead of retreating, they fortified their mountain sanctuary.

It became a safe haven for any soul seeking freedom and deeper knowledge.

As time passed, the attacks grew more violent.

Yet the group expanded rapidly.

Their spiritual abilities blossomed, and their influence spread across the planet.

New leaders began to rise, inspired by their ideals of freedom—just as had happened on Earth and other worlds before. Eve knew the tide had turned.

Nothing could stop the movement of spiritual awakening now.

Her mission was complete—again. I

t was time to return home, to her soulmate.

She prepared for the transition, leaving behind the body she had worn on this world.

Soon, she would awaken at Earth Base, ready for the next stage of her.

19

Attack on the Confederation's Heart

Inside the massive space station—built to endure the crushing gravity of the planet—Fer sat alone in a cargo crate, staring out through the large round window.

His eyes fixed on the last tail star of Ursa Major, the Great Bear.

Beyond it, he knew, lay the Confederation Planet.

It orbited that star—a world that served as the central estate, ruling over seventy-five habitable planets.

Many eons ago, it was here that the alien's vile creatures had won the Great Star War.

Here, they seized power and implemented their insidious plans: domination of all beings through implants and chemical medications.

They turned border planets into prisons for any soul who dared show creative or rebellious thoughts.

But millions of years ago, something extraordinary happened.

Within one of those prison planets, whispers began: someone was teaching that the "natives" were not mere meat bodies, but immortal spiritual beings.

And that it was possible to recover memories of past lives.

As a highly trained officer of the Confederation Elite, I was sent to investigate these dangerous ideas and to erase all evidence—even if it meant annihilating the so-called rebels.

The Eastern mountains—called Tibet by the natives—were ideal for a covert landing.

I hid my single-seat spacecraft at the bottom of an enormous lake before moving toward my target.

Emerging from a wormhole near Venus, I entered Earth undetected.

Wearing the humble robes of a monk and covering my Asiatic face with a yellow cape, I blended among the villagers.

Then I found him.

A small, unassuming man.

But the moment I stood before him, I felt it—the immense, radiant energy surrounding him.

I crept closer, pretending to be another wandering monk.

As night fell, I listened to his words as he wrote by candlelight.

What he said shook me to my core.

He talked of rising above the material universe, of bending physical laws.

Of how we are all immortal spiritual beings, capable of passing from one body to another, carrying memories of our countless lives.

My orders were clear: destroy this heresy. But deep within me, something stirred.

What if everything I'd been taught on Macab, the home world of the Elite, was a lie?

What if I was more than a cog in their machine?

More than a body destined to die and be forgotten?

Conflicted, I returned to my ship, unable to rest.

Flashes of other lives, other bodies, flooded my mind.

When dawn broke, I made my decision.

I went back to confront the small man.

He looked at me with kind, knowing eyes.

I confessed my mission, my weapon ready at my side.

A laser gun capable of disintegrating a body—and trapping a soul at the moment of death.

But he showed no fear.

Instead, he placed a gentle hand on my arm and guided me to sit on a flat rock.

"Do you remember," he asked softly, "a time when you played happily in a green field?"

I didn't know how long we sat there.

Hours?

Days?

But I began to remember.

To truly remember.

I was an immortal being.

Happiness and freedom were possible.

That day, the first spark of rebellion ignited—a spiritual war for the liberation of all beings in this galaxy.

My spaceship still lies hidden beneath that Tibetan lake, a silent witness to the beginning of our fight.

Now, seated in this cargo bay, Fer's gaze lingered on the stars.

Even from this distance, flashes of laser fire could still be seen striking Marcab's fortified cities, where the vile creatures fought desperately to hold onto power.

"One day," Fer whispered, "we will reach our goal.

An universe without war, without slavery, where every man and woman is free to rise to higher levels of happiness and love.]

 Because love is all that matters—love for oneself, for a soulmate, for all that is part of you."

He turned away from the window.

At the door, Eve was waiting for him.

His timeless soulmate.

His eternal lover.

She reached for his hand.

Together, they walked side by side toward a new adventure.

Toward an eternity of freedom, love, and discovery.

END

www.ingramcontent.com/pod-product-compliance
Lightning Source LLC
Chambersburg PA
CBHW061225210726
48294CB00006B/1978